*Cherish your family for they are your treasure.*
*A storehouse of riches...wealth beyond measure.*

Author Unknown

*For our angel and inspiration, Kami*
*To our family and friends,*
*thank you for your continued*
*love and support.*

# WHAT ARE PARENTS?

Written by Kyme and Susan Fox-Lee
Illustrated by Randy Jennings

StoryTyme Publishing
7909 Walegra Road, Suite 112, PMB 178
Antelope, CA 95843
www.StoryTymePublishing.com

First Edition 2004 Printed in Hong Kong

Library of Congress Control Number:  2004092711

ISBN 0-9753699-0-3

SAN  2 5 6 - 0 7 6 3

# WHAT ARE PARENTS? ™

### Written by
Kyme & Susan Fox-Lee

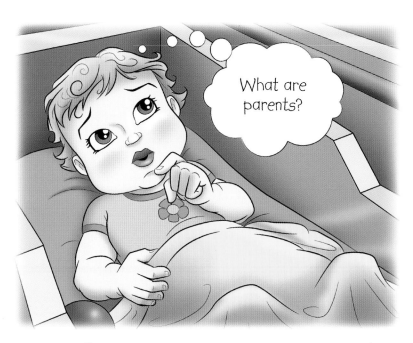

Illustrated by Randy Jennings

On a bright and starry night
when wishes and dreams come true,
a beautiful little baby was born
who looked a lot like you.

This baby was special
as you will see
completing a family
turning two into three.

A nurse came into the nursery that night
to tell the sleeping baby that the time was right.

She whispered softly into the baby's ear,
"It's time to wake up; your parents are near!"

"What are parents?" thought the baby;
the mystery made her grin.

Her journey for the answer was about to begin.

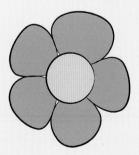

As the nurse and baby walked down the hall,
the baby looked into a room, and this is what she saw.
A mom held her baby, with dad nearby,
cradling their new little one with love in their eyes.

In a room painted with beautiful butterflies,
a family was singing a sweet lullaby.

A song full of love and what the future would bring,
the baby now knew parents love, teach and sing.

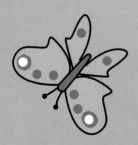

The baby was growing excited; the end of the journey was near.
Filled with anticipation, she knew she had nothing to fear.

Further down the hall a family gathered around their new baby boy.
Sharing their faith gave the parents great joy.

The next room was filled with giggles; the baby wondered from who, then she saw a brother and sister playing a game of peek-a-boo.

The baby heard sounds of celebration
because of the arrival of their next generation.
This young mom and grandma had only just begun
to show their love and devotion to this precious one.

The baby was excited; the end of the journey was here.
Parents love, teach, sing, laugh, have faith and are devoted.
The answer was clear.

As the last door was opened with wonder and delight,
this baby's new journey was about to take flight.

On a bright and starry night, the baby's wishes
and dreams came true . . .

She didn't get just one, but what she got were two.

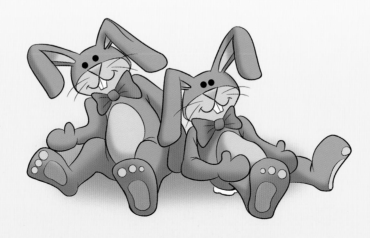

There are all different kinds of families in this great world. Families can be a single mom or dad, adopted children, grandparents as parents and families with two mommies or two daddies.

What makes a parent is someone who loves, teaches, sings,

laughs, has faith and are devoted to their child

# Love

*Love is a hug for no reason.*
*Love is sticky kisses.*
*Love is feeling a tiny hand in your own.*
*Love is endless joy.*
*Love is teaching and learning from them.*
*Love is saying yes and no.*
*Love is pigtails and baseball hats.*
*Love is dandelions picked just for you.*
*Love is that sinking feeling you get*
*when they step out of sight.*
*Love is reading the same bedtime story*
*for the millionth time.*
*Love is me and you.*

Poem by Susan Fox-Lee